Log H

by Liza Charlesworth

ISBN: 978-1-338-84421-4

Art Director: Tannaz Fassihi; Designer: Cynthia Ng; Illustrated by Kevin Zimmer
Copyright © Liza Charlesworth. All rights reserved. Published by Scholastic Inc.

3 4 5 6 7 68 26 25 24

Printed in Jiaxing, China. First printing, June 2022.

■ SCHOLASTIC

It is Dog!
Dog got on
top of a log.

"It is a lot of fun to hop!" said Dog. HOP, HOP, HOP!

3

Fox saw Dog.
Fox got on top
of the log.

"It is a lot of fun to hop!" said Fox.
HOP, HOP, HOP!

Hog saw Dog and Fox.
Hog got on top
of the log.

"It is a lot of fun to hop!" said Hog.
HOP, HOP, HOP!

7

But the log got wet.
Wet, wet, wet!
Then...

Dog got wet!
Fox got wet!
Hog got wet!

Pop saw his sad pals. "It is NOT a lot of fun to get wet," said Pop.

Dog, Fox, Hog, and Pop got on top of the big box.

Read & Review

Invite your learner to point to each short-*o* word and read it aloud.

got

not

pop

on

log

top

dog

hog

hop

lot

fox

Fun Fill-Ins

Read the sentences aloud, inviting your learner to complete them using the short-o words in the box.

> box   Fox   Pop   log   hop

1. It is a lot of fun to _____!
2. First, Dog hops on a _____.
3. Then, Dog hops on a log with _____.
4. "It is not fun to get wet," said _____.
5. Last, the pals hop on a big _____.